Issue # 1

WULFRIC

"WOLF POWER"

CREATED BY
DEION TILLETT

To order additional copies of this book, contact:
Xlibris
844-714-8691
www.Xlibris.com
Orders@Xlibris.com

ISBN: Softcover   978-1-6641-9646-9
        EBook   978-1-6641-9645-2

Print information available on the last page

Rev. date: 10/22/2021

IT WAS A WHILE
BEFORE I WOKE.

OR ENFUSED TO
MY OWN SOUL.

BUT THEN SOMETHING
ABOUT ME WAS ALTERED.

AT LEAST THAT'S
WHAT MY DAD TOLD
ME THAT'S WHAT
HAPPENED.

JUST TAKE IT
EASY SON.

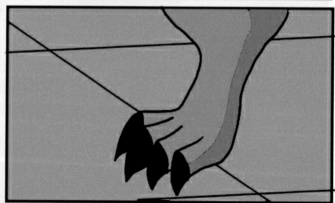

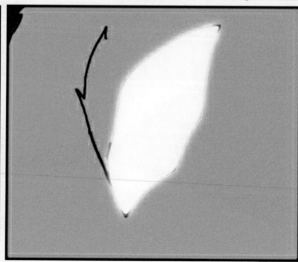

END

AQUILLO COMICS
ISSUE #2
WULFRIC
NEXT ISSUE: "RAVEGERS "
CREATED BY
DEION TILLETT
Deion Tillett

Printed in the United States
by Baker & Taylor Publisher Services